Barney's™ Easter Parade

Written by Guy Davis   Illustrated by Chris Sharp

It happened one Easter,
When *Sammy* and *Sue*
Told Barney why they
Were feeling so blue . . .

"We dyed all our eggs,
We hunted them, too,
And now that we found them,
There's nothing to do!"

Then, Barney appeared
In the blink of an eye!
He said, "Don't be sad,
And I'll tell you why!"

"An Easter parade —
Now that would be neat!
No time for pouting —
Look out at your street!"

They ran out the door –
And what a surprise!
An Easter parade
In front of their eyes!

Flags were a–waving!
Boom! Boom! went the drums!
"Come on!" said Barney.
"The fun has begun!"

"An Easter parade
Means springtime is here!
Flowers are blooming,
And summer is near!"

"Bees are a-buzzing,
Birds flit 'round their nests!
Spring," said Barney,
"Is the time I love best!"

"Let's join the parade!"
And waving his hand,
Barney made his friends
Part of the band!

Sammy played his horn –
Toot! Toot! he blew.
And crash! went the cymbals
Carried by Sue!

"What fun!" Sue giggled,
While Sammy laughed, too.
"Just wait," said Barney.
"There's more fun for you!"

"Look! Here comes a float
With BJ upon it!
There's Baby Bop, too,
In her Easter bonnet!"

"Here comes a new friend –
Hopalong Bunny!
He's a 'Wild West' rabbit –
Isn't he funny?"

"And this hungry bunny
Is Hillary Hopper!
She loves eating carrots,
So don't try and stop her!"

"Here's another friend –
He's a Big Bopper!
He dances around,
This bee–bop hip–hopper!"

"But wait!" said Sammy.
"What's that sound I hear?
Hip–Hip–Hop–Hooray!
Easter Bunny is here!"

He hopped into view,
With a smile so big!
The Easter Bunny
Then danced a fun jig!

With his little bunny vest,
And his little bunny smile,
This lovable bunny
Is always in style!

He loves all children,
So sweet and so dear,
Even though he comes
But once every year.

With a hug for Sammy,
And a kiss for Sue,
The Easter Bunny
Then hopped out of view!

And so, one Easter,
From out of the blue,
Barney brightened the day
For Sammy and Sue . . .

"The parade is over,
But springtime is here!
Easter," said Barney,
"Is a great time of year!"

Barney's Easter Egg Hunt

Written by Stephen White ◆ Illustrated by Aaron Pendland/June Valentine-Ruppe

Early one Easter morning, Baby Bop got a very happy surprise.

"The Easter Bunny came!" she laughed. "See, he nibbled the yummy carrots I put out for him."

"He left us some Easter baskets, too," said BJ.

Barney smiled and said, "Then let's get ready for an Easter egg hunt."

"Do you need any help?" BJ asked Baby Bop.

"No, thank you," Baby Bop answered proudly. "I'm a big girl now."

But Baby Bop's Easter basket was too big.

"Barney," she whispered, "would you please carry my basket?"

"I'd be happy to," Barney chuckled.

"I found an Easter egg!" BJ shouted.

Baby Bop looked up . . . down . . . and all around. Suddenly, she saw something!

Baby Bop said, "I spy with my little eye . . . a bright **red** Easter egg."

"That's not an Easter egg," BJ said to Barney. "That's my red yo-yo."

BJ made the yo-yo spin up and down. But Baby Bop didn't see him because she had already seen something else.

"That's not an Easter egg," Amy said to Barney. "That's my dog's nose."

"Woof," agreed Sadie, wagging her tail.

But Baby Bop didn't hear them because she had already seen something else.

Baby Bop said, "I spy with my little eye . . . a big **white** Easter egg."

"That's not an Easter egg," David said to Barney. "That's a fluffy dandelion."

Barney chuckled as dandelion fluff danced in the breeze. But Baby Bop didn't see it because she had already seen something else.

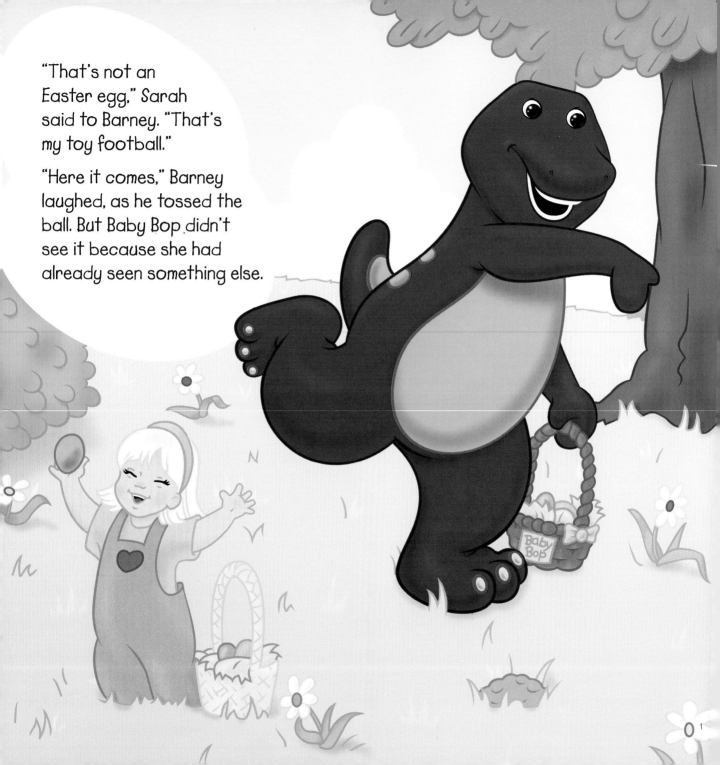

"That's not an Easter egg," Sarah said to Barney. "That's my toy football."

"Here it comes," Barney laughed, as he tossed the ball. But Baby Bop didn't see it because she had already seen something else.

"That's not an Easter egg," Jim said to Barney. "That's a turtle in a shell."

"Happy Easter," Barney said to the friendly turtle. But Baby Bop didn't hear him because she had already seen something else.

Baby Bop said, "I spy with my little eye . . . a shiny **blue** Easter egg."

"That's not an Easter egg," Erica said to BJ. "That's a bubble that I just blew."

Erica filled the air with more shiny bubbles. But Baby Bop didn't see them because she had already seen something else.

Baby Bop said, "I spy with my little eye . . . three bright yellow Easter eggs."

"Those aren't Easter eggs," BJ said to Baby Bop. "Those are Barney's round yellow toes."

Then BJ put some of his Easter eggs in Baby Bop's basket, just like the other boys and girls had done.

Baby Bop looked up . . . and down . . . and all around. "That's all," she giggled. "I think I found all the Easter eggs."

"I spy with my little eye . . . a happy brother and sister on Easter morning," said Barney. And that's just what they were!

"Happy Easter, everyone!" exclaimed Barney.